Lantern Evening

Amanthi Harris

Gatehouse Press

Published by
Gatehouse Press Limited
32 Grove Walk
Norwich NR1 2QG
www.gatehousepress.com

Copyright lies with Amanthi Harris

All rights reserved. No part of this publication may be reproduced, stored in a retrieval system, or transmitted in any form or by any means, electronic, mechanical, photocopying, recording or otherwise, without the prior permission of the publishers.

This publication is sold subject to the condition that it shall not, by way of trade or otherwise, be lent, re-sold, hired out or otherwise circulated without the publisher's prior consent in any form of binding or cover other than that in which it is published and without a similar condition including this condition being imposed on the subsequent purchaser.

ISBN 978-0-9934748-6-6

About the *New Fictions* Pamphlets

The *New Fictions* pamphlets from Gatehouse Press is a series that aims to publish the best new long-form short fiction. Between two and four entries are selected from an open submission process in the 4th quarter of each year; we aim to give a platform both to new writers and to more experienced writers who explore the limits of the short fiction and novella genres. All Gatehouse staff are volunteers, and all profits go back into publishing. For more information, including how to submit work for the current year of the project, see our website: http://www.gatehousepress.com

Body text set in Garamond; titles in Day Roman. Used under licence.

Special thanks to Lee Seaman, James Higham, Livvy Hanks and Natty Peterkin

Cover illustrations by Natty Peterkin, nattypeterkin.tumblr.com
Author photograph by Asher Wolf
Cover design by Norwich Designer
Printed and bound in the UK

Lantern Evening

1.

The month of May was Vesak time – a banner declared it across the North London Buddhist Centre. Ria saw it from the bus on her way to the hospital. Vesak Day always fell on a full moon day and it was the most important date on the Buddhist calendar, the day of the Buddha's birth, death and enlightenment.

If you come out now, we'll light lanterns, she thought to the baby.

The baby stayed very still, hiding inside her. Or maybe it was asleep, rolled tight, squeezed in. It must have been uncomfortable, but still the baby refused to emerge.

'First babies are always late,' people told her, but Ria wasn't so sure. From its intrusive little den inside her, the baby may well have sensed, maybe even seen the barriers in Ria resisting its arrival, tough diaphanous membranes holding back the eruption that threatened. Ria refused to allow herself fear, dousing all tremors of apprehension with tranquil images from her hypnosis CDs: deep sheltering woodlands, sunset beaches, a stone cottage in the mountains with a log fire. She read poems and articles about the extraordinary fulfilment of motherhood, and willed on her own feelings of motherly bliss. Anything to shield the baby. She couldn't risk it glimpsing the horror she'd felt as the stick-test turned positive, even as Rob kissed her over and over. Those terrible thoughts might still lurk in her, anxious flickering flares racing along her nerves, alerting the waiting child in the red glow of her interior.

Poor baby.

She wanted it to have as cosy and happy a time inside as those babies of mothers who had always wanted them, who had their love ready and waiting like newly-papered rooms with animal stencils, a mobile hung over the cot.

The baby moved after its long stillness. Had it just woken from a nap, or had it lain watchful and curious? Fearful? It made a watery ripple inside her, raising an arm maybe, or extending a curled-up leg.

Hello, baby. Good afternoon. We're on our way to see the nice nurses. Nothing serious, they just want to check that we're okay. Did you know it'll soon be Vesak?

She thought of tissue paper lanterns in the dark of mango trees in her childhood garden. It was always the lanterns in the gardens she thought of, not the dazzle of electric lights in the streets of Colombo or the temples ablaze with festivity.

The gardens looked like Fairyland, Baby. At night we drove around looking at them with my grandfather and grandmother- your great-grand parents... oh gosh, Baby, I wish they were here with us now, if only they could be...

Again and again these days, that first life drifted up from where it had once lain calmly forgotten. Tears spilled, dripping openly down her cheeks, unstoppable. How much she wanted to have back what had been lost. It was about to be lost again, she sensed, but with far greater finality. The baby would start a new clock, its own new childhood begun. Ria would keep watch over it, turned away from the one past that had mattered until now. She had to let go of it. She hid her face from the people on the bus, hid the fury and sadness in her.

Don't be scared, baby. It's okay, I'm fine. I'm just missing them, that's all. Anyway, on Vesak Day, the three of us- no four,

Lena, my ayyah, came as well. We'd go to the temple next door and say hello to the priest, then go for a drive in Grampa's car and look at all the neighbours' gardens.

But the memory ended there. Only the one Vesak remained, her last in Sri Lanka – the year her grandparents decided to take sil and sit piously all day on low stools at the temple, praying and meditating and eating only once before noon like the monks. That same year, Lena and Cara the cook went back to their villages for the holidays and only Ria and her parents were left in the house. What a Vesak to remember.

2.

The day before that Vesak Day, Ria's father, Mahesh came home from work with a box of paper lanterns, the type called buckets – cylinders of coloured tissue paper with a wire rim and wire handle.

'The simplest type,' Laksmi, Ria's mother noted, watching from the veranda. 'And the cheapest.'

She didn't lower her voice. Mahesh may have heard her. He left the box on the back seat of the car and came into the house empty-handed. He didn't mention the lanterns. No one did. But the next morning, after breakfast, Mahesh went up onto the flat-roof and strung wires between the washing-line posts and the water tank and he fetched the box from the car. Ria followed him up to the roof and stood close as he took out a pale green lantern folded flat.

'You put the candle inside like this,' Mahesh said prising the folds apart.

The lantern glowed in the sun, the colour of lime boiled sweets that Grampa kept in a glass jar in his wardrobe and shared after lunch. Ria unfolded a red lantern, fixed a candle in the silver stand inside, and her father hung it up. Ruby-red and lime-green swung side by side bobbing companionably in the sea breeze. Trees rustled as the breeze came inland. At the temple next-door, speakers put up for Vesak crackled to life and blared out prayers, drowning out the muezzin's calls from the mosque over the road.

'The priests' revenge,' Mahesh said, and they both laughed.

In the neighbours' garden, the children played. Ria didn't call out to them, feeling distant and mysterious up on the roof, looking down at the three girls running after their little brother, trying to pull him off his tricycle. There was a smell of spices and wood smoke. A group of women were preparing lunch while next-door's cook, dressed all in white and taking sil like Ria's grandparents, sat placidly disengaged on a bench. Footsteps sounded on the stairs. Ria knew without looking that it was her mother.

'It's so hot!' Laksmi exclaimed, staying at the top of the stairs. 'You'll burn, Ria. Go inside.'

Ria chose another lantern, pretending not to hear. Purple. Laksmi didn't march over to slap her for disobedience or drag her downstairs to lock her up. Ria had known she wouldn't, not with Mahesh there.

'We're going to Mona's at seven,' Laksmi told Mahesh.

'Is that a question or a statement?'

'It's anything you want it to be.'

'And what about all this?' Mahesh reached for the purple lantern and hung it up.

But Ria hadn't pushed the candle in far enough. The candle fell over inside, making the lantern tilt. The sun filled its emptiness, making it gleam the colour of grapes in her Aesop's Fables – the grapes the fox longed for and finally hated.

'If you don't want to come to Mona's, that's fine by me,' Laksmi told Mahesh.

'But you're going?'

'Of course I'm going to my sister's for Vesak. And they've invited us to see their new Yamaha organ. I'm sure Ria would like to see it – wouldn't you, Ria?'

Ria hated Laksmi, hated knowing that an answer wasn't required.

'After all,' Laksmi added. 'It's the closest she's going to get to one. Isn't it?'

'Then she must see it. I do hope you've accepted their invitation.'

Laksmi said nothing. She went downstairs. As always it wasn't clear to Ria who had won the argument. She watched her mother's legs, body, the top of her hair disappear, and the lingering unease of her cold hurt gaze. Mahesh removed the purple lantern from the line and shook out the fallen candle. He squashed the lantern flat and threw it into the box, kicking the box as if by accident.

'There are more important things in the world. Life isn't just about having Yamaha organs,' he said severely. 'But that's all that matters to you, isn't it?'

She twisted inside, ashamed, muddled by feelings she didn't know to express, that he wouldn't have understood anyhow. She longed for him to know that she preferred any day, hands down, the battered old piano her grandparents had bought her for her ninth birthday, but she didn't hate Mona's world, and he knew that about her.

Mahesh headed for the stairs.

'Come in now,' he ordered.

He waited. The red and green lanterns swung cheerily on the line, unaware of having been abandoned. She eased the purple lantern open, smoothed its crushed folds, and replaced the candle, this time pushing it in hard. She held it out to Mahesh. His anger wavered. He came back and took the lantern from her and hung it up. She took out another: lemon yellow and put in its candle. He shook out an orange one, the colour of jelly. She chose a pink next, a deep fuschia, like popsicles – the ones a man sold from a basin of ice, that she wasn't allowed to eat in case they were made with tap water. Silently she and Mahesh worked and one by one the lanterns went up until there were none left.

That night, showered, scented, dressed for the evening, they ate dinner together, a cool tense peace arisen between Laksmi and Mahesh the way it did when the release of other people lay ahead. Laksmi's sandals clicked impatiently on the driveway as they went to the car. Ria sat in the dark behind them, excited now at the thought of Mona's world waiting up ahead. A rich cocoon to be embraced by, the real evening soon to begin.

    All along the lane, lanterns glowed in gardens, pulsing colours in the black foliage. Their spread across the neighbourhood was broken only by the quiet of Tamil and Muslim houses with the curtains drawn, only porch lights on. Up on the main road, lights flashed from giant pandols with painted scenes of the Buddha's life. Even the fountain outside the ice-cream parlour was beaded with electric bulbs changing from red to blue to pink to green, back to red again. Palm-thatch dhansalla huts had been built on the pavements and were filled with people eating food donated by the families who lived nearby. Ria looked out for the big pots of lentil dhal and yellow rice that Cara had cooked before leaving for her village. Laksmi pointed out decorations on the roadside to no one in particular. Mahesh drove in silence.

3.

There were no Vesak lights on Mona's road. The large white houses, even of Buddhists, were as muted and discreet as ever behind their high walls. Hem, Mona's husband, had declared Vesak lanterns to be fire hazards so at Mona's the only lights on outside were the garden lamps under the Cholea plants glowing coolly through the leaves and a spotlight on a Japanese stone pagoda. A maid opened the front door and Ria and her parents stepped into the hall with its polished black floor, a Chinese lacquered cabinet bearing a mahogany lamp with a tasselled shade, giving out a serene amber light.

'Hello, hello, we're nearly finished, come and sit!' Mona called from where she, Hem and Ria's two cousins, Pri and Shoba, were still seated at dinner.

Hem and Mona were hardly ever at home, always having to attend social functions, but now they sat relaxed and casual, Hem in a striped silk sarong, not trousers, and an emerald-green silk shirt, pristinely pressed. Mona wore a navy blue kimono, her hair down in a loose plait, not drawn into its usual chignon.

'Tell the maids what you'd like to eat,' Hem told Ria and her parents.

'We've eaten already,' Laksmi said.

'Something to drink then?'

'Thanks. Whisky,' Mahesh requested.

'I meant something soft, it being a Poya day. But there is whisky if you'd like it.'

'Yes, please. I'm sure Lord Buddha will understand.'

Hem went to the drinks cabinet while Laksmi glared at Mahesh. Mona called to the maids to bring Nescafes for everyone else. Laksmi went over to the new organ. It was draped in an old curtain, cream with red roses that had once hung in Mona and Hem's bedroom.

'Can we take a look?' Laksmi asked.

'Of course!' Mona beamed. 'Just take off the cover, have a good play!'

Mahesh sat down and picked up a newspaper and started to read as Laksmi lifted the flowery curtain.

'Sha!!' she cried. 'This is really something, Akka!'

'It's good, no?' Mona came to stand by her, tall and stately, by far the more majestic of the two sisters.

They had both had piano lessons when they were younger, but it was Mona who had learned to play well. The two gazed at the double-keyboard and rows of red, yellow and green switches for making the organ sound like other instruments: a trumpet, oboe, flute or clarinet.

'I'm so happy with it!' Mona said. 'It's a much better model than our last one.'

She flicked a switch and played a few notes in a quick arpeggio, her big pale hands spread wide, rings glittering. Then she burped. Very loudly. But maybe because Mona was tall and pale-skinned and beautiful, it didn't seem like bad manners; no one even seemed to notice.

'Why don't you play something?' Mona asked Ria.

'Yes, go on,' Laksmi urged. 'But play something you know. No mistakes please.'

Ria sat on the stool. It was made of the same hard brown plastic as the organ. Below her skirt it felt cold against her legs, its edges sharp.

'I hope your hands are clean,' Pri said.

'Of course her hands are clean!' Laksmi retorted. 'Why? You think we're dirty? Just because we don't have a big Yamaha organ?'

'Now, now, my goodness!' Mona winced. She hated ugliness of any sort in her home.

'Pri is only concerned because this is a very precious item. So please, Ria darling, go and wash your hands.'

Ria slid off the stool.

'What for?' Laksmi challenged Mona. 'She had a bath before she came. She's only been in the car. There's no need for her to wash her hands again.'

Laksmi gripped Ria's shoulders, keeping her close, yet Ria didn't feel protected or claimed.

'Pri, why don't you play something for us?' Hem said.

'That's a good idea.' Mona brightened. 'You watch how Pri does it, Ria.'

'Any requests?' Pri asked, sitting on the stool and adjusting its height, turning a large round chocolate-coloured knob. She tossed back her long ringlets.

'Do you know *Ma Bala Kale*?' Mahesh asked.

'*Ma Bala Kale*?' Pri spluttered laughing and Shoba joined in.

It was an old Sinhala song, wistful and sentimental, about someone remembering sitting on their mother's knee. It was old-fashioned and unstylish but Ria had heard her father sing it when he thought he was alone in the garden and sometimes at night on the back balcony.

'Uncle Mahesh, you really must get more with it!' Pri said.

'That's the kind of thing he likes,' Laksmi muttered.

Mahesh went back to reading his newspaper, while Pri played Nights in White Satin to a bossanova beat and Hem and Mona looked on proudly. Laksmi listened with Shoba, nodding in time. Then the maids wheeled in the dessert trolley and everyone returned to the table for Nescafes and fruit salad and chocolate biscuit pudding.

'Now you all eat, please,' Mona told the maids.

'Isn't it time for the fireworks?' Hem asked.

'The fireworks! Of course! I almost forgot!' Mona called the maids back. 'Girls! Let's get the fireworks ready, please! After that you can have your dinner in peace!'

The maids ran into the garden and Pri snapped off the power to the organ. Shoba helped her cover it with the old curtain.

'Come, Ria!' Mona said as Ria lingered by the organ. 'It's fireworks now. You can play later.'

'Yes come, Ria!' Laksmi said. 'Leave that bloody thing.'

She took Ria's hand and pulled her over to where Mahesh sat. He remained absorbed in the sports pages.

'You're staying here? Why do you always have to cause a scene?' Laksmi hissed. 'Come and see the fireworks.'

Strangely obedient, he folded the paper and came with them to the porch and stood to one side, facing the dark garden. His pale face that people said was handsome was expressionless, watching Hem instruct the maids to hammer in Catherine wheels onto the gatepost and rockets into the lawn. Ria wondered if Mahesh was wishing he was with his own sisters, they who made barbed little jokes about snooty City folk, and said how like her mother Ria was, in distinctly unfriendly tones. Mahesh never told them to stop, he never stood up for her, acting as if he hadn't heard. On the other side of the steps, Laksmi sat with Mona and Pri discussing the society people they knew and their antics. Shoba joined in, pretending to know what they were talking about. Hem finally strolled over to Mahesh in his dark corner and they talked about cricket scores.

The maids nailed the last Catherine wheel to the gate and struck a match. They stood to one side and watched with the family as the fireworks sparked and whirled and whizzed, bright flashes shooting into the sky over the quiet cul-de-sac. Ria thought of the bucket lanterns waiting on the flat-roof. There was still time for them.

But once the fireworks were over, they went inside and the Nescafes had grown cold but there was extra dessert: chocolate eclairs, a coffee gateau from the famous Green Cabin restaurant, chocolate ice cream from Elephant House. Then Pri played a medley of Bond theme tunes, and only after that did Ria and her parents leave for home.

4.

In the city, the streets were quiet. In the dhansalla huts men sat eating leftovers. On Ria's lane, the lanterns in the neighbours' gardens had gone out. Nero, their guard dog, woke in his kennel as the car drove past, gave them a cursory bark and settled down again to sleep. Even the festive chanting next-door had ended and a silence had fallen over the temple. Ria longed for Lena to come running out, to take her up to bed eagerly demanding news from Mona's house as she helped Ria to undress. But that night an empty house waited. Ria followed her parents upstairs.

'Quick, brush your teeth, then pyjamas,' Laksmi said.

'What about the lanterns?' Ria demanded.

'We'll have to light them some other time. Now it's bedtime.'

Laksmi went into the main bedroom and switched on the bedside lamps. The blue walls glowered, the fan came to life and the door closed behind her. Mahesh went out onto the back balcony. Ria stood in her doorway with the distant patter of her mother showering and on the balcony, Mahesh silently looking down into next-door's garden. Then Mahesh climbed the stairs to the flat roof, the firm steady step of his leather chaporas, drawing Ria outside. She climbed the stairs, the cement banister smooth under her hand, still warm from the day's sun. Over the parapet she saw Mahesh sitting on the edge of the water tank, the lanterns ghostly shadows shifting in the breeze. From the way he was leaning back against the wall of the water tank, gazing at the sky with its powdery stars and round full moon, she could see that he wasn't angry anymore. She went and stood between his knees, looking out with him at the night time world of the neighbourhood. The coconut trees sighed in the winds turned stronger, wilder at night, stirred by the churning sea beyond the main road. On the other side of the garden wall, the temple buildings huddled in darkness. In the dormitory the priests would be sleeping, peaceful under old sheets worn thin with washing, rows of bald heads on soft lumpy pillows. Behind her, her father sang:

> '*Ma bala kale*
> *Amma-ge ukule*
> *Nalavunu thale*
> *Mata thama sihiwe…*'

His voice was soft, playful, he went on singing, letting her be there with him, leaning back against him. And the world felt gentle and kind and right. He felt it too. Ria could tell.

5.

At the hospital check-up, Jo, the midwife on duty, seemed more concerned than in the previous week.

'Have you been running?' she asked. 'The baby's heartbeat seems a little raised.'

'Do I look like I can run?'

Jo smiled. 'Well, make sure you get lots of rest. You'll be needing it very soon.' And she squeezed Ria's hand. All these past months, the midwives' goodwill had never faltered; their sweet pure kindness urged her on. Ria never doubted their sincerity, their pride and belief in her to successfully grow and contain a whole baby, held her safe.

'Let me check the baby's heartbeat again,' Jo said. She leaned over Ria, listening intently. 'It's gone down.' Jo straightened, relieved. 'Maybe it had a little wriggle earlier – I'll check your blood pressure again as well.'

The band inflated, constricting her arm. Ria stroked the great bulge of her belly.

Don't panic Baby. We'll be fine. Don't get stressed.

The pumped up air hissed out.

'Your pressure's gone down,' Jo said. 'Were you feeling anxious earlier?'

'Maybe. A little…'

Ria gazed from the bed out to the hospital rooftops, to buildings where the sick were kept away from the women with babies. A giant chimney rose against the blue of the sky, where smoke would puff out at times from burning the dead – no, not the dead, dirty dressings full of pus and blood and sheets soaked in vomit and excrement. Yet dying and sickness seemed far away from the peaceful peach-coloured room with matching floral curtains, the simple sturdy machines in the corner for checking on labour.

'I feel so calm here,' Ria said.

'We're all here for you. You're going to be fine,' Jo said. 'We can leave it for a few more days without intervening. But let's do another scan just in case.'

Ria walked along the sun-dappled corridors of the Birth Unit, a view of a serene, far away London outside. Midwives passed her on their way to other rooms, other women. Through doors Ria glimpsed blotched faces, un-brushed hair, a woman in a blue dressing gown slumped in a chair, an older woman cradling a blanket-wrapped baby. Another woman lay with a small pink head pressed feeding to her pale heavy breast. The midwives smiled at Ria. Some stopped to hug her, proving she was one of theirs, one of their protected, one of their Mothers. But soon an actual baby would require her to be an actual mother and she would have to become one somehow.

No one knows what it'll be like, Baby. You have to trust me. And I have to trust you.

The baby kicked out a leg, shifting discontentedly. It wanted more reassurance; wanted to know what lay ahead.

How can I tell you, Baby? Even I don't know. There's no one to ask.

6.

Her mother had been shocked to hear the news. Ria had known to expect it, which was why she had waited three months to tell her, and why she hadn't invited Rob to their lunch. Ria hadn't wanted him to witness Laksmi's reaction, always so honest, so brutal. But why shield Rob at this time when it was she who was supposed to be at her most vulnerable? Why not have him present to guard her and fight off the attack of an assailant determined to undermine, to destroy? Yet what Ria had feared most was Rob seeing in Laksmi's reaction a likeness to Ria's own, reminding him of the naked dismay that Ria had let show as the third stick test turned to YES. She needed to believe that Rob had forgotten, that his brain had suppressed the memory of that moment. Chemicals, perhaps, of fatherhood quenching it to allow him to go on believing her a good mother for his child.

'Are you sure it's not a false alarm? You've done a second test?' Laksmi demanded.

'I've done several.'

'They all said the same?'

'Yes.'

Ria had even gone to the doctor who had refused to do more tests – the ones from the chemist were highly accurate these days, Ria had been told. And in any case, by the time Ria met Laksmi she had already had her first scan – something she didn't mention. The picture of the little head with the nose that turned up exactly like Rob's, the giant stomach that the doctor said was completely normal, was in the pocket of her Moleskine diary, to be taken out and studied in quiet moments. It wasn't to be exposed to the glare of Laksmi. So many words of Laksmi's had lingered in Ria never to be shaken out – until that is, the baby's arrival. The presence of the baby had changed things. It had cleared Ria's mind. Old fears had disappeared, maybe obscured by the silky skeins of hormones and new concerns – the new knowledge to decipher about caring for a child. The old voices in her had faded. Ria felt the peace of their absence. She wanted only to prolong the quiet, to allow this strange easy distancing from her life before and the life going on around her. A whole other world had sprung into being inside her. That was enough for now.

A world begun from the time of that first scan and seeing the baby swimming inside her, its thin legs kicking furiously, then a moment later floating on its back, its tiny tongue shooting out to lick the placenta –

'It's finding ways to amuse itself,' the consultant had told her and Rob. 'You have a little character in there!'

The doctor had laughed with a gentle affectionate pleasure in their creation. Could happiness really be so unwilled? So accidental? Rob, inexplicably, was in tears and smiling blissfully and she too had welled with a fearful excitement. She had clutched Rob's hand while he kissed her and decided in that instant to ride this new challenge and to enjoy it the way she imagined other women did. She would rid herself of regrets, the longing for a life missed, thwarted and the fury in her at being denied – all this she let sink down in her without remedy. Perhaps it had passed out dissolved in urine, the new urine, with the baby's mixed in with hers. She had expelled it from her and she was revived and pure; new for the baby.

7.

It was three months after their lunch when Laksmi next called Ria – to tell her that Pri and Shoba were in London, visiting.

'They're staying in a flat near Regent's Park. They've invited us to tea! Girls only, I'm afraid! Rob will have to do without you!'

The flat was in a mansion block, nowhere near the park but still obviously an expensive address. The lobby had marble floors and brown wallpaper and a doorman who barely looked up from his desk as Pri and Shoba buzzed them in, shrieking down the stairwell:

'Helloo! We're on the second floor. Do you need to take the lift?'

Ria and Laksmi climbed the stairs to Pri and Shoba standing at a door.

'Oh my God, Ria, you're huge! You look like a bus!' Pri cried.

'You're ready to pop!' Shoba giggled.

'Please don't have the baby here, just think of the lovely cream carpets!'

Pri and Shoba were dressed alike in a confection of tweed jackets, shirts with ruffles, jodhpurs and shiny lace-up boots, their take, Ria guessed, on upper class British horsey fashion. Pri looked over Ria's jeans and clogs with quiet disdain and a certain smugness.

'How far gone are you?' she asked.

'Six months.'

'Three more months? Oh my God, you won't be able to move by then!' Shoba shrieked.

'I'm not that big.'

'Yes you are!'

'And you've put on weight around the face,' Pri said.

They went into a sitting room full of beige leather sofas, gilt chairs, a gold-legged glass coffee table. They stood, Laksmi gazing in awe around her, staring up at an oil painting of an unsmiling Asian couple posed in that very room.

'That's a portrait of Shankar's uncle and aunt,' Pri said. 'They hardly ever use this flat, we've got it for as long as we like.'

'Are you here for work?' Ria asked her.

There was an exchange of looks between Pri, Shoba, Laksmi, a secret communion. A sign of recent conversations, confidences, outings even, perhaps to which Ria hadn't been invited.

'I didn't tell her,' Laksmi said.

Of course you didn't, Ria thought. For once the stab of betrayal failed to arise in her. But what was it that Pri and Shoba possessed to make Laksmi so much happier with them than with her own daughter? How could a mother feel distrustful of her own child? Was it something that accrued over the years, or did it happen at birth? Could it start earlier?

'I'm here for some treatment,' Pri said.

'Are you ill?'

There was nothing in Pri's red glossed lips, gelled wild curls, eyes dramatically lined with kohl and shadowed with shimmering pinks to suggest ill-health. Was it something sinister hidden inside her, something that had invaded, something to fight against?

'Fertility treatment,' Shoba announced.

'Wow.' Ria said. 'That's – amazing.'

She didn't know what else to say; 'good luck' seemed too cruel. No one wanted to be reminded of chances and probabilities, the uncontrollability of this particular success. Ria glanced at Laksmi, but clearly she wasn't concerned that Pri was actually choosing motherhood. There was no reminder that her career might be halted or fatally altered, that her life would be taken over, her independence severed irrevocably. Had Laksmi secretly decided that IVF was unlikely to work in Pri's case as Pri was about to turn forty? Or did Laksmi imagine Pri better suited than Ria to being a mother?

'I have no intention of getting too big if I get pregnant,' Pri declared. 'I've told Shankar I'll be working out right to the end.'

'You'll break the machines!' Shoba sniggered.

Pri flicked a Windsor Castle tea towel at her.

'You should work out more,' Pri told Ria.

'I do yoga.'

'Pregnancy Yoga, right? But that doesn't do anything for the physique, it's just a lot of women huffing and puffing, I know, my friend used to go. She stopped after two weeks and got herself a trainer. You should see her, Aunty, she's got a body to die for. Two days after giving birth, she looked like a model.'

'Don't you worry Pri, you'll stay glamorous even when you're pregnant,' Laksmi assured her. 'You'll be like one of these film stars you see in the papers.'

'And Kate,' Shoba added.

'Kate? Kate who?'

'Middleton! Really, Aunty! We know more about your Royals than you do! Didn't you see how she looked just hours after birth?'

'I didn't much like the dress, it was far too old for her. She needed something more funky,' Pri declared. 'But high heels, all credit to her! Somehow I can't see you in high heels hours after you give birth, Ria!'

'You wouldn't have seen me in high heels before I was pregnant, either,' Ria retorted and Pri smirked, agreeing.

Ria sat on the nearest leather sofa, sinking into the cold stretched skin. She drew a beige chenille cushion to her, hugging its softness against her belly, smothering out sound for the baby. But would it still hear their joyless prattle and sense the kernel of hardness at the centre; no silent unspoken affection to soften it, or to lift those taunting words; no shared pleasure in each other.

Baby it's not right to stay in a room with people who don't make you happy. It's not silly to want to feel good with other people, to feel cared for and wanted.

Ria took out her phone and glanced at the time.

'What is it? Did someone call? I didn't hear your phone ring,' Laksmi said accusingly.

'Just checking my messages. There's nothing.'

There actually was a text, from another mother-to-be, asking how Ria was. And here was another new discovery, this world of gentle strangers who knew the most intimate things about you, people who shared your fears and were grateful for the smallest acts of kindness. She basked in the comfort of her new world, among the women swollen and waiting, preparing like her for a new life to begin. In a few minutes she would say she was tired and call for a taxi to take her home.

This, by the way, baby, is not the best way to escape such situations – it would be far cleverer to know in advance not to bother, to make up an excuse and not waste a perfectly nice Saturday evening while your daddy gets to stay at home watching television.

She wouldn't mention Rob, she wouldn't mention that she wanted to be in her own home, to be with him. Why tell them what they already sensed, that he was her true family now, so much more than them.

8.

A few days after meeting Pri and Shoba, Ria drafted and re-drafted an e-mail to Mahesh:

'I'm going to have a baby.'

She had calculated the right time to send it: Sydney was ten hours ahead of UK time.

'Congratulations,' he replied.

Six hours later. And by email, not a phone call out of the blue as she had let herself imagine, half hoping, half dreading it. But the news hadn't jolted him enough for that. Then, silence. In the days and weeks and months that followed he hadn't thought of anything to add.

9.

Rob arrived at the hospital, just in time for the scan. At first the baby was facing into her but when it moved it was only to turn away from the ultrasound probe. The baby curled in a new configuration, fists covering a round grumpy face, puffed cheeks. Its long skinny folded-up legs filled the screen, then it turned again and a bottom pushed up at them as if in protest.

The senior midwife had come with them.

'The baby's fine, but it's getting bigger all the time. We can't leave it in much longer,' she advised. 'Shall we try and induce you? A very weak dose to begin with? Just to get you started?'

'Just a few more days! The baby isn't ready yet,' Ria pleaded.

Couldn't they see? Couldn't they tell? Did that defiant little being look like it wanted to leave its safe warm nest?

They walked down a leafy street, to where Rob had parked the car – yet another of their new purchases for the baby's arrival. Before the baby, they had been happy to take the Tube and buses everywhere. Now they sat side-by-side alone together, Rob driving them home. She asked him to go past the Buddhist Centre, the way the bus had gone.

'You took the bus? Are you crazy? You have to take a taxi if you go anywhere now. You do realise the baby can come at any time?'

But that wasn't likely. The baby had no intention of coming out, not now, not yet – the baby knew better than anyone what she was feeling inside. It knew her unreadiness.

Nothing prepared you for motherhood, other mothers said, those who knew. It came at you, whether you liked it or not. Still, a threshold had to be crossed and there was no going back for things left undone, unknown, things she would need on the other side.

The Vesak banner blew above the gates of the Buddhist Centre.

'You want to go in?' Rob asked, slowing the car.

'Maybe just to take a look.'

They parked in a road of small restaurants with white linen covered tables, cosy and close, set mainly for two. It would be a while before they could go again to such restaurants, a while perhaps before she wanted to – would she ever again want those quiet dinners, just the two of them talking of plans and dreams, the lives they longed to live?

On the gate of the Buddhist Centre was a poster announcing an evening of silent meditation, no mention of fireworks or lanterns. It sounded stark yet dignified, suited to the celebration of a day of transition: birth, death, enlightenment. She had not known before why those three separate events in the Buddha's life should have been bound into one occasion, but now she understood; they were all the same: fear marked each of them, such final, irreversible passings with no chance of return, with only the possibility of regret.

The Buddhist Centre was actually a house. Although the gate was open, the front door was locked. There was a bell to ring. They rang it: Ding! Dong! It made the sound of doorbells on television sitcoms. Nobody answered it. Someone else arrived – a man in a raspberry red woolly hat and matching jumper. He had a key.

'Are you here to see someone?' he asked.

'We saw the sign about the festival,' Rob said.

'Ah, the celebrations – it's all on the website.'

'You're not open every day?' Ria asked.

'In the evenings we are, for meditation. You can book a course of six sessions. All the details are on the website.'

It was not a temple. Even if it were, it could never have been like the temple next-door that you could go into at any time, through the gate in the garden wall built when Ria's grandfather donated part of his land to the monks order. Lena would take Ria with her at sunset time, and in the months after the driver ran away with a maid from Mona's house and Lena grew melancholy, they went during the day sometimes as well, stepping into the cool of plantain trees at the edge of the temple garden and walking barefoot on the sandy ground to the priests' house, to the head priest seated on the veranda. They bowed at his feet while he murmured a blessing over them and afterwards Lena would have the same lostness in her eyes as earlier but she would seem consoled going back to the house, holding Ria's hand in hers, keeping her close.

Was it a blessing Ria had wanted, coming to the temple in North London? Like Lena crouched before the head priest, being blessed as she faced the new uncertainty ahead? But there were no priests at the North London Buddhist Temple, only Westerners, like the man in the woolly hat and jumper, who lived ordinary lives with families and jobs, who had ordained themselves and wore special sashes on special occasions. There was no blessing to be had from them.

Ria and Rob headed home. She lay on the bed while Rob made raspberry leaf tea for bringing on contractions and the room filled with the stench of burning sage oil that the midwives had suggested she try. Ria's birthing CD played into the quiet of this unfamiliar daytime, of life suspended, waiting for the unknown, their life as they had known it about to change forever.

'...visualise your pelvis,' instructed the voice on the CD, a famous Indian gynaecologist.

She had the drawl of educated-Asians, the accent her cousins affected in Colombo, even Mona sometimes, when she was with her society friends. The doctor sounded like an aunt – not Mona – a generic aunt, or a friend of the family, come over to advise; caring, concerned but uninvolved, not needing to judge or interfere. The doctor's words passed into Ria, down through her limbs, surrounded her belly that was so filled, so solid, yet pliant and tender; a pumpkin, a giant apple gleaming in the sunlight slanting in past the blinds.

'Your pelvic bones will soften and become the consistency of unset jelly. Your baby will glide through... soon you will hold it in your arms.'

The doctor prepared her and all the other women listening in bedrooms all over the world, following her words, willing their bodies to obey her. Ria knew she would survive whatever came next. She would be strong, she would soften and yield to the passage of the baby, down through her jelly pelvis – so what was stopping the baby from starting its descent? What was the baby waiting for?

Ria climbed the stairs twenty times each hour, ate two pineapples, burned more sage oil and finished all the raspberry leaf tea, but the baby barely moved, disdainful of the potent molecules sent to destabilise its cushioned existence. The telephone rang. It was Laksmi.

'Any news?' Laksmi sounded excited.

She had gone to the theatre with Pri and Shoba. Laksmi was always excited taking visiting family into Central London, to the theatre. Showing off her London and the West End shows that were so much better than anything they had in Colombo, and finding restaurants unlike any the others would have seen before. She had a favourite cocktail she always ordered, served with a red glacé cherry on a stick and she was giggly and vivacious, how she might have been in Colombo if it hadn't been for Mona always there to push into the centre. In London Laksmi was a little girl in a frilly dress, a big bow in her hair, laughing and loud in the circle of family, far away from Mona. Far away too from the suburbs and dullness of everyday life. Was it only in London that one paid this price for being close to the lights and music and dancing? Or was life anywhere merely a series of exciting spikes in an otherwise uniform blandness, the entrapment worsened by having children?

'No news,' Ria said. 'How's the show?'

'It's amazing! You'll have to try and see it, the costumes are unbelievable! Here – you can ask Pri and Shoba all about it.'

The roar of the theatre bar at interval time rushed in as Laksmi switched the phone onto Speaker.

'One thing, Nicole Kidman can't sing for toffee!' Shoba yelled.

'Shush, Shoba!' Pri scolded.

'She can't hear! She'll be in her dressing room.'

'But she might have friends in the audience. There's press everywhere.'

'Maybe I'll get quoted.'

Not one of them mentioned their non-appearance at Ria and Rob's flat the previous evening.

'I thought you were coming to our place for tea yesterday,' Ria said, unwilling to let them get away with it too easily.

She would have been expected to explain if she hadn't turned up after promising to visit – and it was an effort she and Rob could have done without, at a time when they should have been relaxing.

'We tidied the flat and bought cakes and ground coffee especially –'

The speaker was switched off abruptly, and there was the scuffle of Laksmi grabbing the phone and scurrying away perhaps from the others, then silence. Ria sat with her legs propped up on a stool, watching the sun set beyond the plane trees, a glowing orange streak above the neighbourhood rooftops. A squirrel ran along the pavement below, past a knotted plastic bag of dog poo that someone had dropped.

'Really, Ria, you could be a little more sensitive,' Laksmi said breathlessly. 'Do you think it's easy for Pri to see you pregnant while she has to undergo treatment?'

'One phone call, just to say you weren't coming, that would have been nice.'

'I don't think you appreciate what she's going through – do you realise she has to inject herself everyday with hormones? A huge injection into her leg. She has to inject it herself, it's a massive needle, I've seen it, I could never do it. I never realised how brave she was until now. And there's no guarantee of success – in fact she's been told her chances aren't very good.'

'And that's why you didn't call?'

'I have to get back, the bell has gone,' Laksmi said impatiently.

'Enjoy the show. You don't need to keep calling. I'll call you if anything happens.'

'Fine.'

The phone snapped off. Once there would have been a void, an ache, an inky black anger simmering in her all night. But now the sage-scented calm of her world filled the void. She leant back on the sofa. Rob brought her a plate of pineapple. They chose the hottest curry on their favourite takeaway menu, chose a DVD. It was hard to imagine a London with people dressed up and tottering in heels to restaurants and clubs, sipping cocktails at a bar, talking on and on about the people they knew, the lives of the relatives dissected. So many people scattered around the world, people that the baby would one day have a right to know. But there was time for all that.

You need to come out Baby. Don't be put off by these people. Families are messy most of the time but we won't be, I promise you. We will be careful. We will think before we act. We won't hurt you. We will find our way to the right people. At the very least, Baby, we'll try.

But there were no guarantees. Nothing prepared you for who you would be on the other side of the birth that you prepared for so meticulously. A mother should reassure, but a mother working blind, working in trajectories of hope, extrapolations from ideals of the mother she would like to be

– a mother so precariously equipped was likely to scare anyone off. What an unappealing prospect for the baby. It seemed dangerous even to her.

10.

That night she lay awake while Robert slept, and only then did the baby grow restless, sending vague watery ripples of movement through her.

What are you doing in there, Baby? Is it time? Are you ready?

Ria heaved up from the bed and went into the sitting room. The moon shone over the houses opposite. A pale full Vesak moon. She sat on the sofa gazing up at its unreal milky glow.

Baby? What's the matter with you? Why don't you come out? Are you scared?

She pressed in the side of her bulge and something pushed back firmly. She checked the messages on her phone. There was nothing from Mahesh. She thought about sending him a message, a question requiring an answer. But she couldn't think of a single question to ask – and in any case, why should she? He didn't care. He wasn't interested in what happened to her. She had every right to ignore him for another twenty years. But soon it would be morning and the midwives would be on the phone again. It seemed important to speak with him before anything happened; she did have a question she wanted to ask. She watched the clock, watched the pulsing colon between minutes and hours. Time was running out.

'The baby is due. So shall I keep you informed of progress?' she texted.

A new opening. Seconds later he texted back:

'Is your mother going to be helping?'

She tensed. Here was a genuine enquiry, not a platitude, and founded on facts that he and she shared.

'Mum's still getting used to the idea,' she returned.

She also typed: 'in her own inimitable way,' but deleted the words straight afterwards. Mahesh had never let her criticise her mother to him, scrupulously avoiding any accusations that he'd colluded with Ria. Ria had always known that she was alone with her mother, left together on their side of the split.

'Children ruin your life,' Laksmi had told her many times, in the years when the two of them were cooped restless and trapped in a tiny damp flat in the suburbs of Middlesex. Ria then had wanted only to return to Colombo while Laksmi strove each day to erase her connection to that very place, the source of all betrayal and shame and the oppressive presence of Mona that she had longed all her life to escape.

'For a woman, having children means never doing what you want,' Laksmi said. 'You can just give up on your dreams when you fall pregnant. Your career is shot once they know you have a child and then you have to take what you can. For men it makes no difference, they get to carry on just the same.'

Ria pressed the green telephone symbol next to 'Dad' and Mahesh's number came up on her phone. In Sydney it was the afternoon. Was he at work? Did he still work? Was he drinking cold lager by a pool? Playing golf? Had Sandra begged him to stay away from the one daughter they didn't share, a daughter from another time, before their life together? Sod her, Ria thought. I bet Sandra's the reason why he hasn't called. Ria pressed dial.

'Hello? Ria?' Mahesh answered. 'What time is it there?'
'One A.M.'

'Are you okay?'

'I was just sitting here thinking,' she said. 'Do children ruin your life?'

'No.'

The right answer. Not even a pause to think. It was the conventional answer, the other, one couldn't say out loud – at least not to most people, not if you wanted them to stick around. Mahesh was a conventional person – that much had emerged after he had left her mother. Sandra was a normal wife, sane and stable with modest aspirations, a teacher, happy with her job, not straining for impossible heights and undefined pinnacles of success that eluded most people. They had a house in a cul-de-sac and two calm quiet daughters who said very little the one time Ria met them, many years ago. They were probably dull but he must love them, to reply as he had, straight-off, with no hesitation.

'Don't listen to your mother,' Mahesh said. 'She never understood anything. Her family only cares about money. And when's that ever made anyone happy?'

Possibly he was right. Pri, after all, for someone married to a millionaire businessman seemed surprisingly discontented. But Shoba was happy, thriving in her work at a leading television station and resolutely single, dating on occasion with no strings attached.

'I'm like Aunty Laksmi,' she declared. 'She's the one who has the best time.'

Ria wasn't like her mother or her cousins, but they were not the only people in the world. There was another possibility. It hadn't appealed before, yet now it stirred in her, a new foundation unearthed, to settle against, to nestle into.

Would it be so bad, so reeking of defeat, to align herself with Mahesh's world?

'Do you remember our last Vesak?' she asked him.

A pause, full of unease on the other end of the line. She heard him clear his throat.

'I have good memories of it,' she assured him quickly.

'Listen Ria, let go of the past. Move on. A new life is starting for you with this baby – it's a totally new beginning – take it, make the most of it.'

He was talking about himself and his other life; the wife and the children he had chosen to keep, to own.

'A baby is a whole new chapter,' he said.

He sounded like someone in a bad book. Or an episode of Neighbours.

'So you don't remember our last Vesak?' Ria asked.

She hated him. He had never understood. Anything.

'You don't remember what happened afterwards?' she demanded.

'Afterwards? After what?'

'After Vesak night at Mona's.'

'Oh God! That night! Christ. How could I forget? Well, I can tell you now, I suppose, that was the night I knew.'

She wanted to agree, to say, wild with gladness and relief: yes, me too! But she didn't.

'I just knew I had to end it. That evening was the last bloody straw, that was when I knew I had to get out, for all our sakes.'

But mostly yours, she thought. And at last she understood the gladness and relief, the lightness in him that had made him so gentle and yielding that night.

'How much is this call costing you?' Mahesh asked. 'Have you arranged a special tariff?'

'No.'

'You can get these cards now, you use them to ring abroad really cheaply – even with a mobile phone.'

'Yes, I know.'

'Next time get one. You can get them in any mobile phone shop, even in the street people are handing them out sometimes.'

'Okay.'

'You'd better get off the phone now. Anyway you need the rest. Thanks for the call. Good luck. Let me know how it goes.'

She pressed a button and he was gone.

11.

Ria leaned back on the sofa looking at the moon's chill whiteness. Its brightness throbbed. For once the road below was empty, no Police sirens passing, no flashing blue of ambulances silently racing with the sick and terrified inside. The silence settled around the room, the shelves of her books, a red rug on the pine floorboards, a farmhouse table that she and Rob had bought in a junk shop and stripped and oiled and polished themselves. On the table a vase of cornflowers – the wild cornflowers she loved, small and blue, such an improbable colour after the red, orange yellow-gold brightness, the magenta and pinks of the flowers she had grown up with – cornflowers that Rob had bought for her that morning with the pineapple. This was the world she had made. It was strong, it could hold her, it could hold all three of them.

Baby? Are you awake? I'm sitting on the sofa, waiting for you. So hurry up. Daddy's waiting for you too.

She sang to it:

*'Ma bala kale
Amma-ge ukule
Nalavunu thale
Mata thama sihiwe...'*

What it means, Baby, is: when I was young, how I was soothed on my mother's lap, I still remember it.

And she did remember. Mahesh had been filled with hope and all the joy of release that night, it had made him full of love and gladness for the moonlit night. She remembered the gentleness of his hand on her back, his voice softened and lingering on the notes as he sang to her as she stood between his knees. It was a perfect moment. It need never be tied to the rest of what happened, or what he chose to recall – it was hers too, not just his – hers to have, exactly as she wanted it. That single moment, unaltered, touched by the same moon, travelled across continents and time back to her.

> *'Ma bala kale*
> *Amma-ge ukule*
> *Nalavunu thale*
> *Mata thama sihiwe.'*

The baby shifted and stretched, flexed muscles; testing, preparing. Love was a fact, love existed, even when it didn't reach another person. There was love in that solitary moment on the flat roof with the unlit lanterns. It was hers to remember, to keep, to give. She cupped her hand around her belly, letting the baby know.

Acknowledgements

For J and K with love.

I am very grateful to Gatehouse Press for selecting this story for the New Fictions Prize. Thank you to Sam Ruddock for edits and encouragement, to Andrew McDonnell, Meirion Jordan and to Martie De Villiers who always sees the first draft.